D1142340
B48 233 657 8 SLS
SCHOOLS LIBRARY SERVICE
MALTBY LIBRARY HEADQUARTERS
HIGH STREET
MALTBY
ROTHERHAM
S66 8LD
MAR 2005
ROTHERHAM LIBRARY & INFORMATION SERVICES
This book must be returned by the date specified at the time of issue as the DATE DUE FOR RETURN.
The loan may be extended (personally, by post or telephone) for a further period if the book is not required by another reader, by quoting the above number / author / title.
LIS7a

For Jo, with all my love.
T. B.

To Sam.
R. B.

First published in Great Britain in 2004 by

Gullane Children's Books
an imprint of Pinwheel Limited

Winchester House, 259-269 Old Marylebone Road,
London NW1 5XJ

1 3 5 7 9 10 8 6 4 2

The right of Tony Bonning and Rosalind Beardshaw to be identified as the author and illustrator of this work has been asserted by them in accordance with the Copyright, Designs and Patents Act, 1988.
A CIP record for this title is available from the British Library.

ISBN 1 86233 548 6

Printed and bound in China

Snog the Frog

Tony Bonning • Rosalind Beardshaw

Beside a grand and
majestic castle was a pond,

and at the bottom
of this cool, clear pond
lived Snog the Frog.

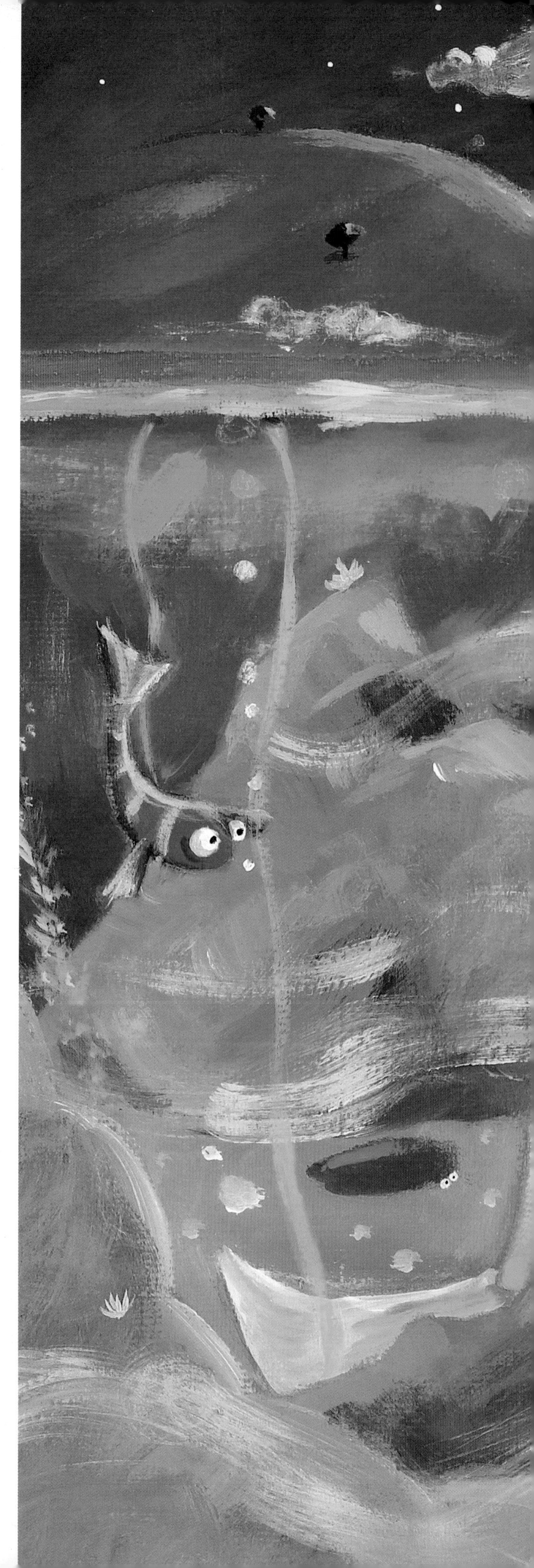

Snog the Frog climbed on his log and said,
"Today is St Valentine's Day, and today I wish to feel like a prince. And to be a prince I need a kiss!"

With that in mind, he leapt onto the land and went

HOPPITY HOPPITY HOPPITY HOP,

until who should he meet, but Cow.

"Oh Cowy Cow Cow! I wish to feel like a prince.
Pucker up your lovely lips and give me a kiss!"

"Who? You? Moo! No! Now go!"
"Oh! Just one?"
"No, go!"
And with that he went . . .

HOPPITY HOPPITY HOPPITY HOP,
until who should he meet, but Sheep.

"Oh Sheepy Sheep Sheep! I wish to feel like a prince. Pucker those luscious lips and give me a kiss."

"Me? Meh! Baa! Nah! No!"

"Oh! Perhaps a peck?"

"Nooo, go!"

So with that, Snog the Frog went

HOPPITY

HOPPITY

HOPPITY HOP,

until who should he meet,
but Snake.

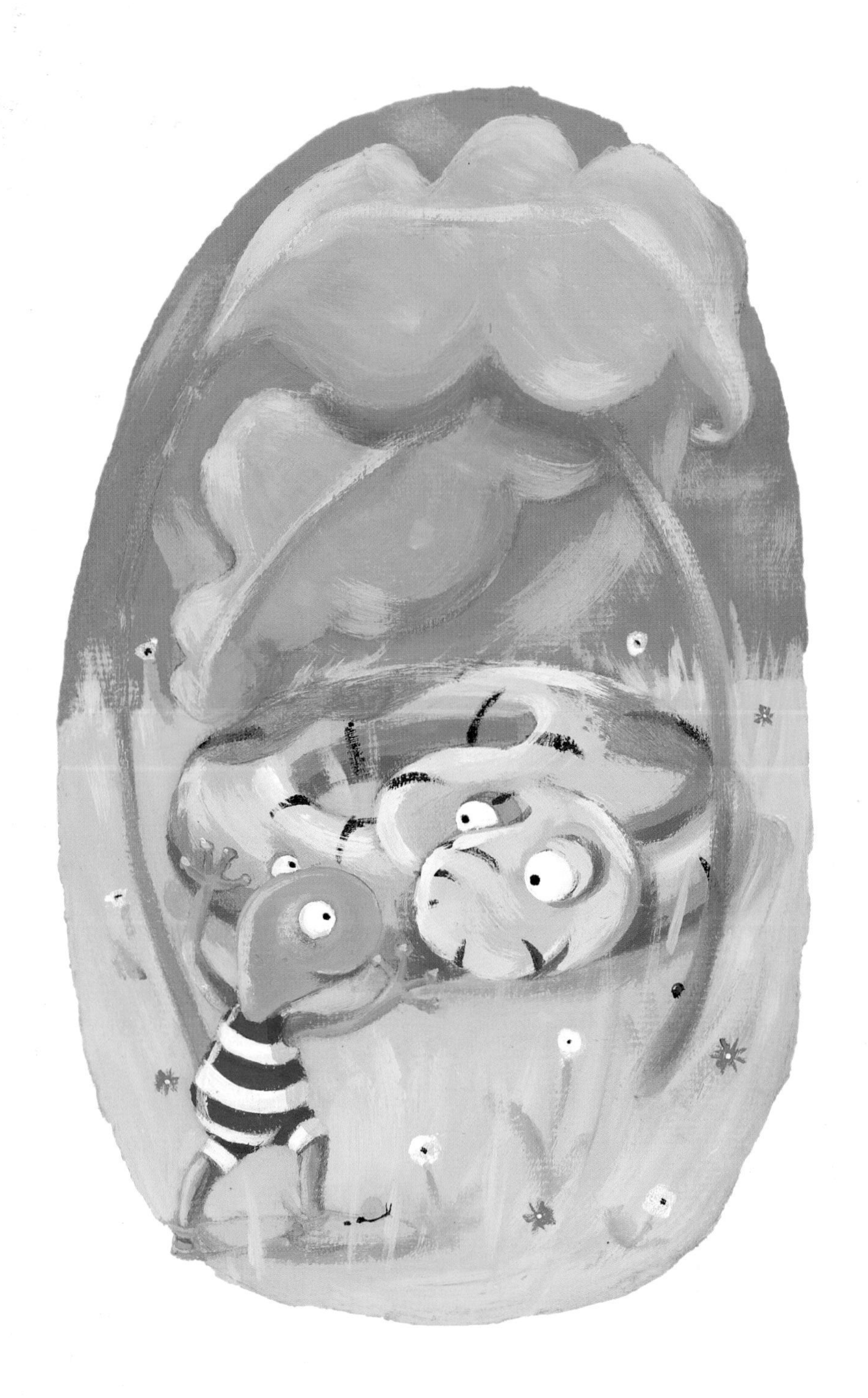

"Oh Snakey Snake Snake! I wish to feel like a prince.
Press those lean lips on mine and give me a kiss."
"A kiss, hissss, take this!"
"Oh no! I'll give that a miss."

And with this, he went HOPPITY HOPPITY HOPPITY HOP, until who should he meet, but Pig.

"Oh Hoggy Hog Hog give this Froggy Frog Frog
a snoggy snog snog."
"What! Snort! I'd never kiss your sort."
"Spoilsport."

And with that, Snog the Frog went

HOPPITY

HOPPITY

HOPPITY HOP,

until who should he meet, but . . .

...Princess!

"Oh Princess, Your Highness, such happiness would I possess were you to kiss me but once. Make me feel like a prince."

"Oh!" said the Princess, "I've read about this in the Fairy Tales. One kiss and you turn into a prince."

And with this, she lifted Snog the Frog
and gave him a kiss.

"Alas, something is amiss.
The kiss has not turned you into a prince."
"Again, again, just one." The deed was done but . . .

nothing!

"Oh my!
Have one last try."
She did.

"I have tried once
and twice more since,
but you have not
become a prince."

"**No!**"
said Snog the Frog . . .

“But I feel like a prince…
and that’s the main thing!”